WOLVERINE™

AN ORIGIN STORY

Based on the Marvel comic book series Wolverine
Adapted by Rich Thomas Jr.
Illustrated by Val Semeiks *and* Hi-Fi Design

New York

marvelkids.com

TM & © 2013 Marvel & Subs.

Published by Marvel Press, an imprint of Disney Book Group. No part of this book may be reproduced or transmitted in any form or by any means, electronic or mechanical, including photocopying, recording, or by any information storage and retrieval system, without written permission from the publisher. For information address Marvel Press, 114 Fifth Avenue, New York, New York 10011-5690.

Case Illustrated by Pat Olliffe and Brian Miller
Designed by Jason Wojtowicz

Printed in the United States of America
First Edition
1 3 5 7 9 10 6 8 4 2
G942-9090-6-12335
ISBN 978-1-4231-5401-3

Many years ago, in the heart of the Canadian wilderness lived a savage animal.

The **wolverine,** as it was called, was small, but fierce.

It liked to be alone, but ventured out to hunt
for game when it felt hungry.

It was stout, but quick.

Others lived here, too, on an estate amid the wilderness.

Children: **JAMES. ROSE.** And a boy nicknamed **"DOG".**

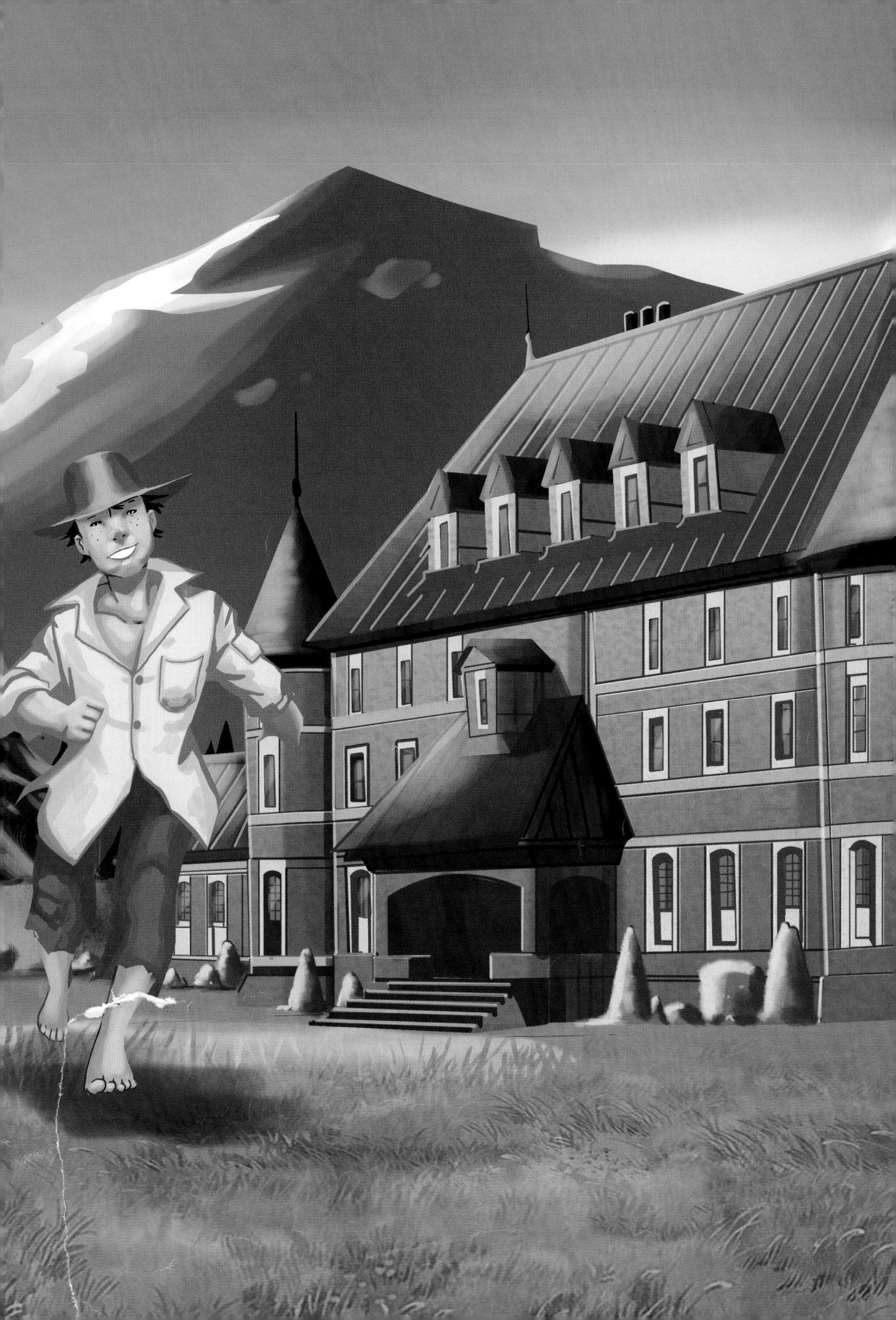

Dog's father, **LOGAN**, lived there, too. He was the groundskeeper.

And the estate belonged to young
James's father, John Howlett.

James had a brother. But in those days people did not know as much about science or medicine, and his brother had died.

The estate had felt like something was **missing** since he'd been gone.

And no one felt this way more than James's mother. She rarely left her room, and did little besides think about **James's brother.**

This left her little time for James.

But for all the sadness in the big place, **James had happy times there, too.** Mostly with his friends Rose and Dog.

They played together, worked together—

—grew up together.

But Dog, whose father treated him badly, **became mean** as he grew older.

And Dog began to **dislike** James . . .

. . . in the same way the groundskeeper disliked James's father.

And one night . . .

Dog and his father broke
into the Howlett home and
sneaked upstairs.

They were angry and jealous
and wanted to fight.

James felt scared, and angry too.

And suddenly his hands started to feel **strange.**

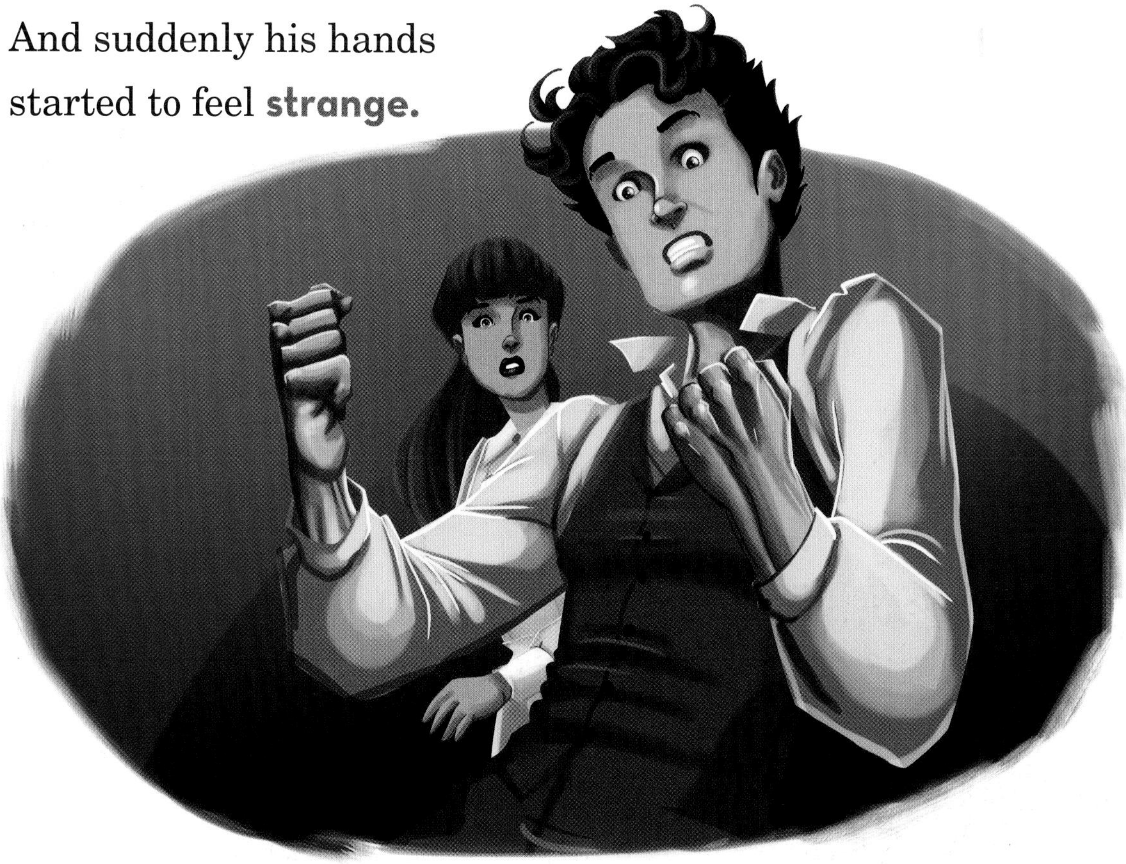

He needed to defend his family and his friend Rose.

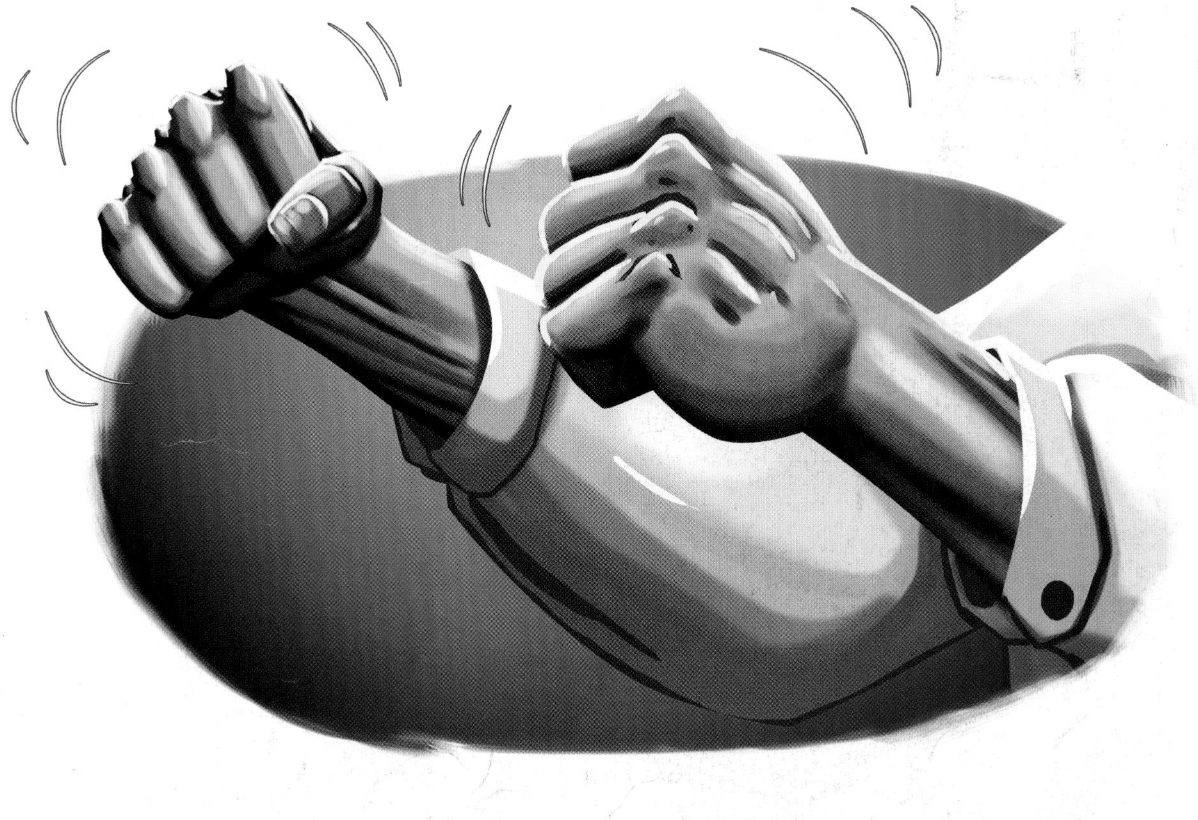

And without warning, James discovered he was something **more than human . . .**

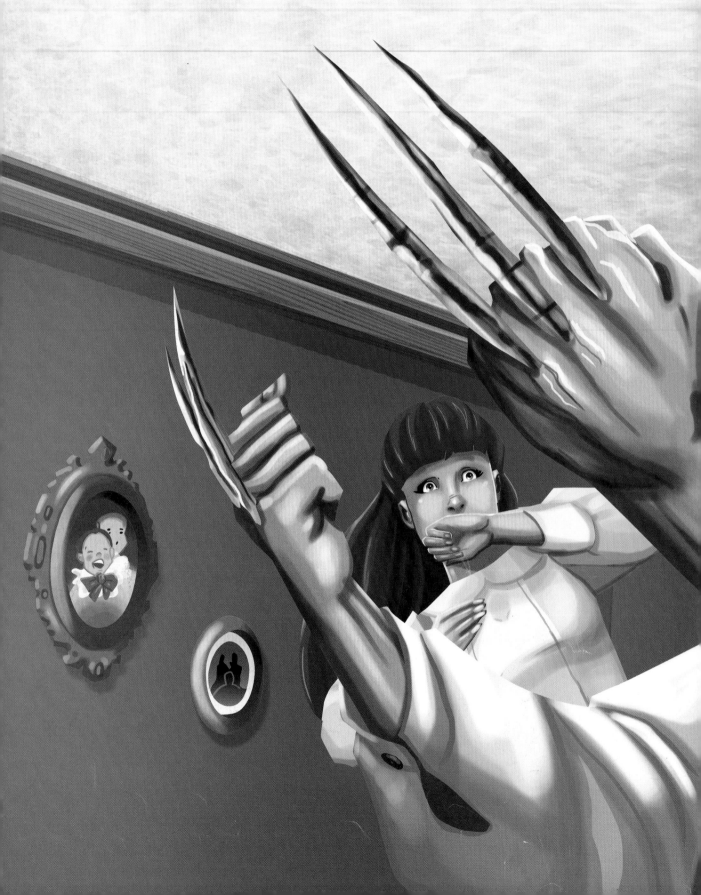

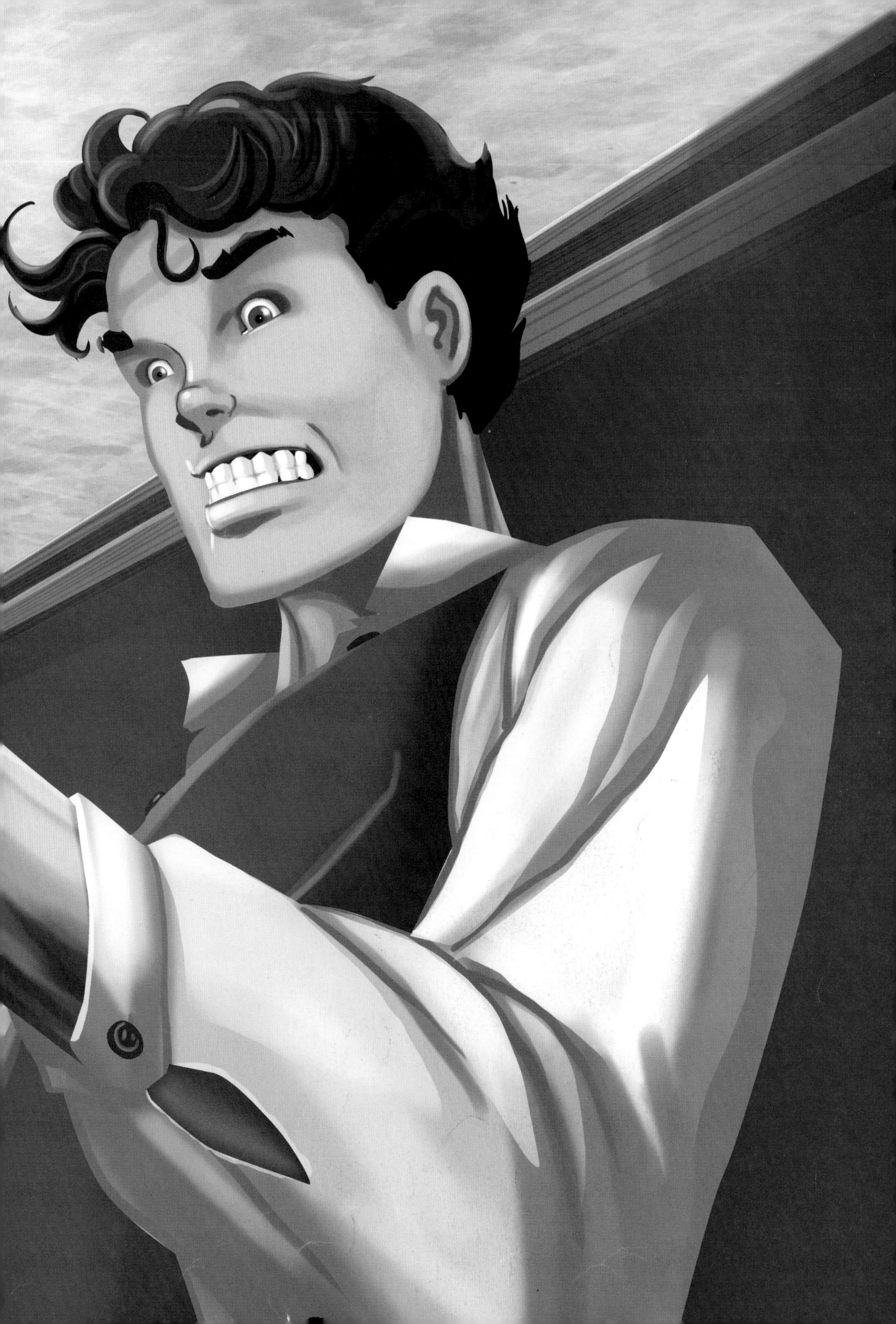

. . . but Rose knew people might
see James as something **less.**

She grabbed James by the wrist

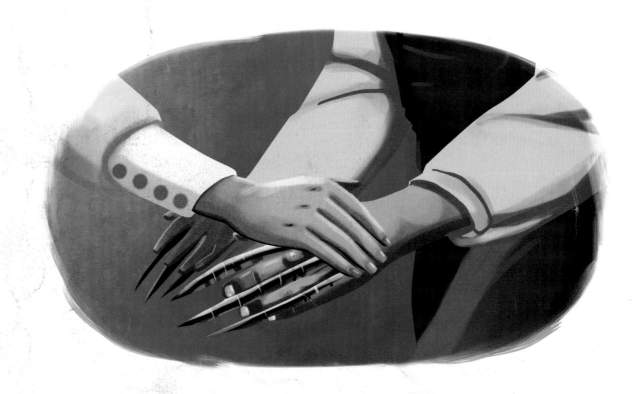

and ran from the house.

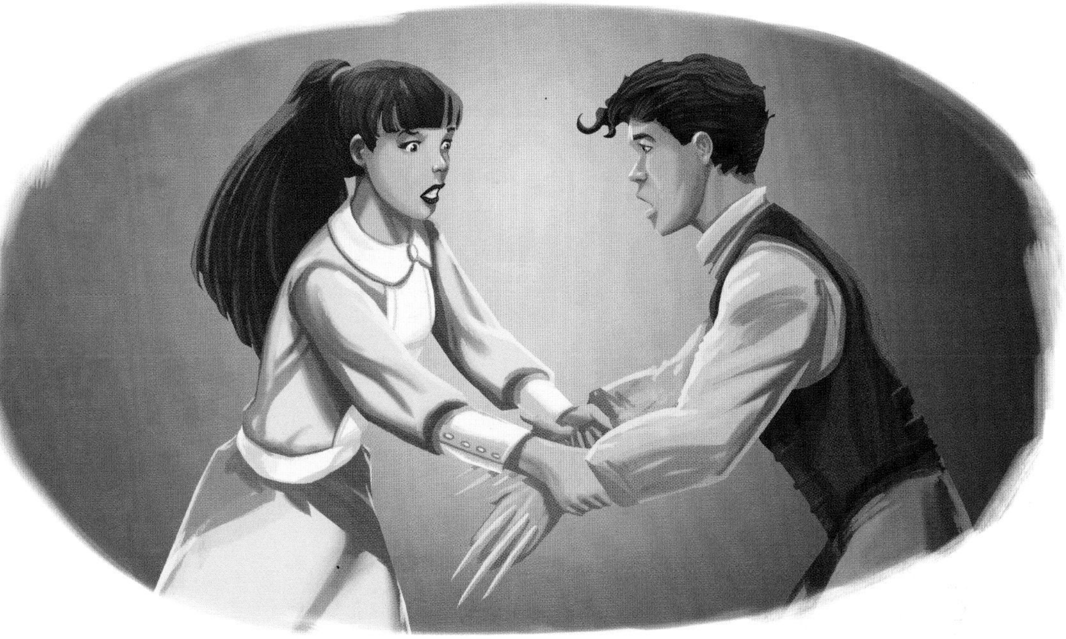

James couldn't save his family, but **Rose could save James.**

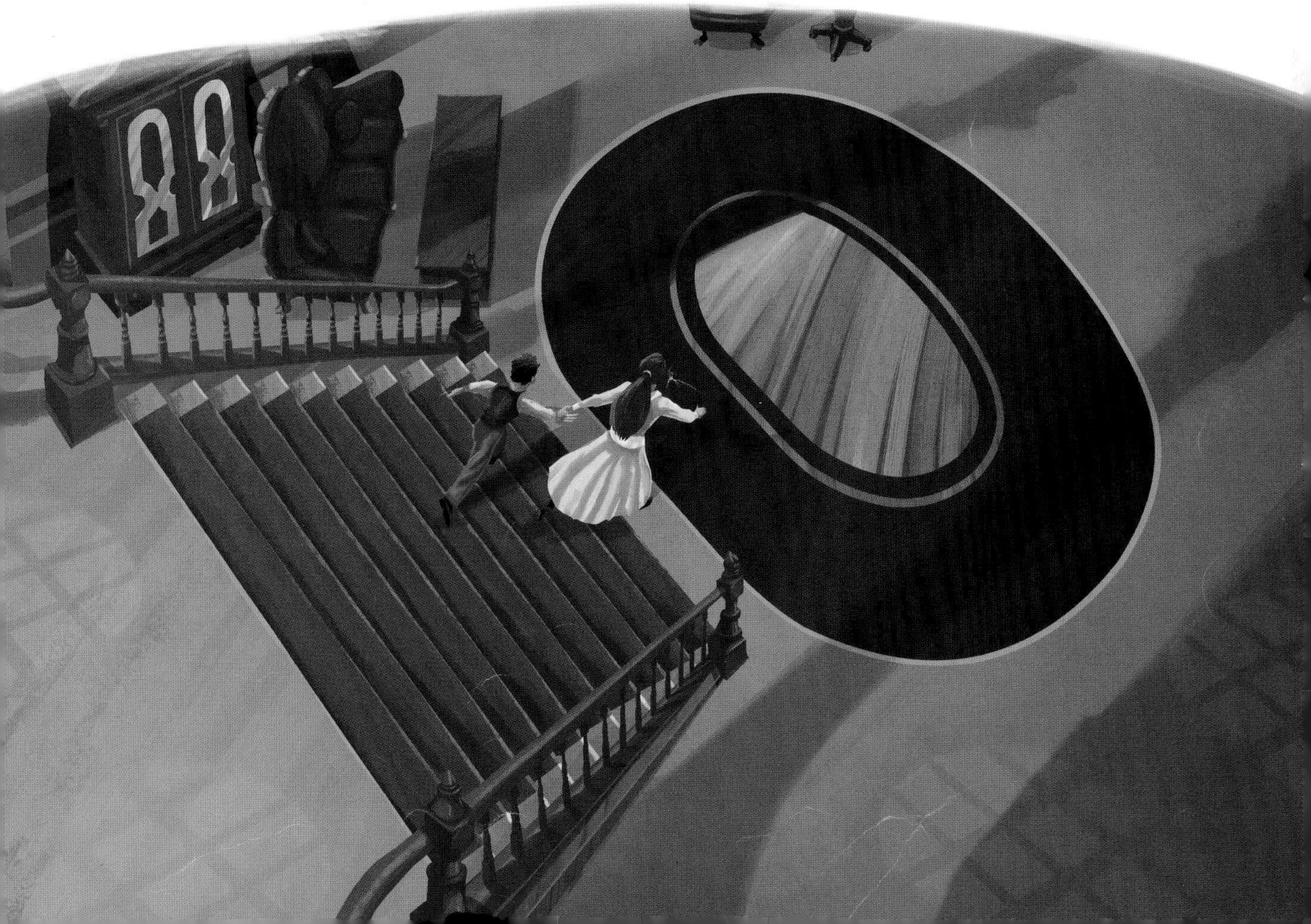

She took what they needed

and sneaked aboard a train.

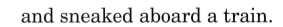

They needed to go some place
no one knew them.

Some place no one would hurt
James.

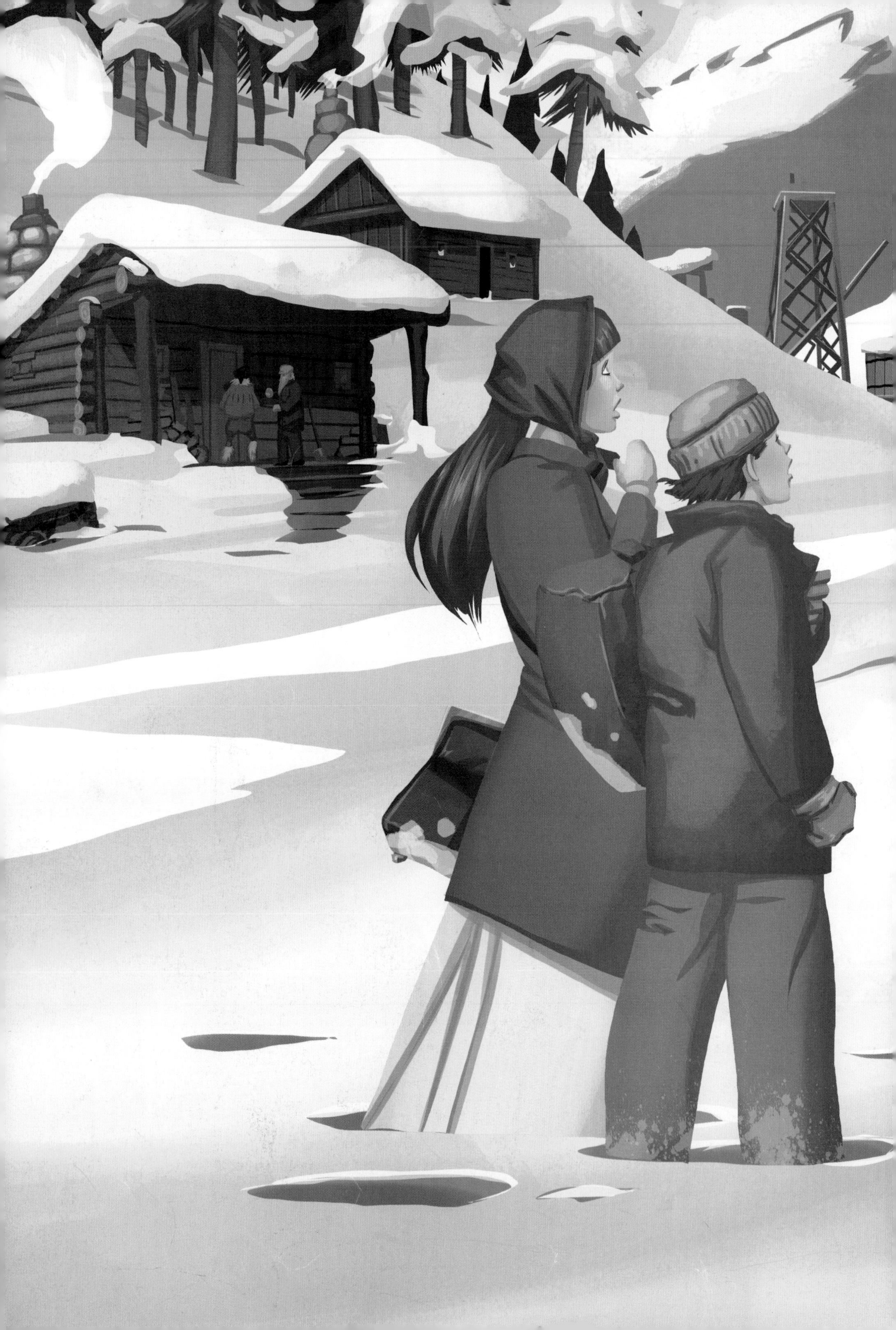

They arrived in a mining town, and met a man named **SMITTY** who was the head of a work site.

Smitty told James to remove his gloves—he wanted to see if his hands were good enough for working.

Rose was scared. She thought Smitty would see James's wounds from his claws, or worse, the claws themselves.

But when James removed his gloves, **there were no scars.** Even though it seemed impossible, James had healed!

In order to keep their secret safe, Rose told the townspeople that James's name was Logan.

Logan took some hard knocks.
But always picked himself up.

And as Logan grew up, he eventually
left Rose and his old life behind

and learned to control his abilities.

Logan also learned to be strong, stand up for himself and others, and **always do what he knew was right.**

Not only did he still have claws and the ability to heal easily, but Logan also learned that he had an **animal's senses.**

He could see, hear, taste, smell, and feel as well as a wild animal.

Logan loved being in the wild, and for a time
he left behind his life at the camp to live there.

Time continued to pass, but **James didn't grow much older.** His healing factor kept him young.

He left the woods, and began to travel the world.

He fought in a great war.

And then he fought in another.

And during peacetime he settled in Japan.

Upon returning home, **Logan was kidnapped!**

The people who took him hooked him up to a machine. They knew that his **healing factor** would help him survive their experiment.

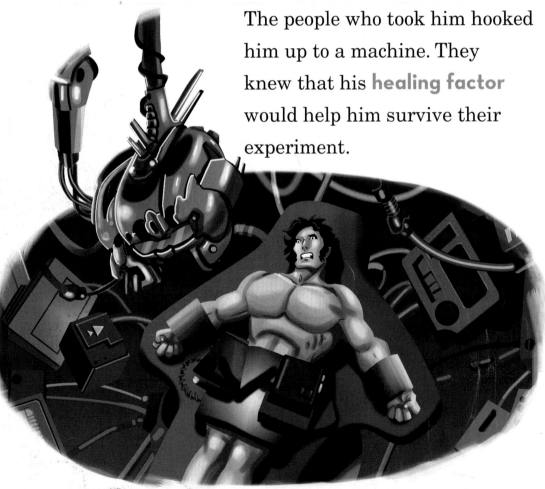

They erased his memory and coated his bones—and his claws—with an unbreakable metal called ADAMANTIUM!

Logan managed to escape
into the forest.

He ran . . .

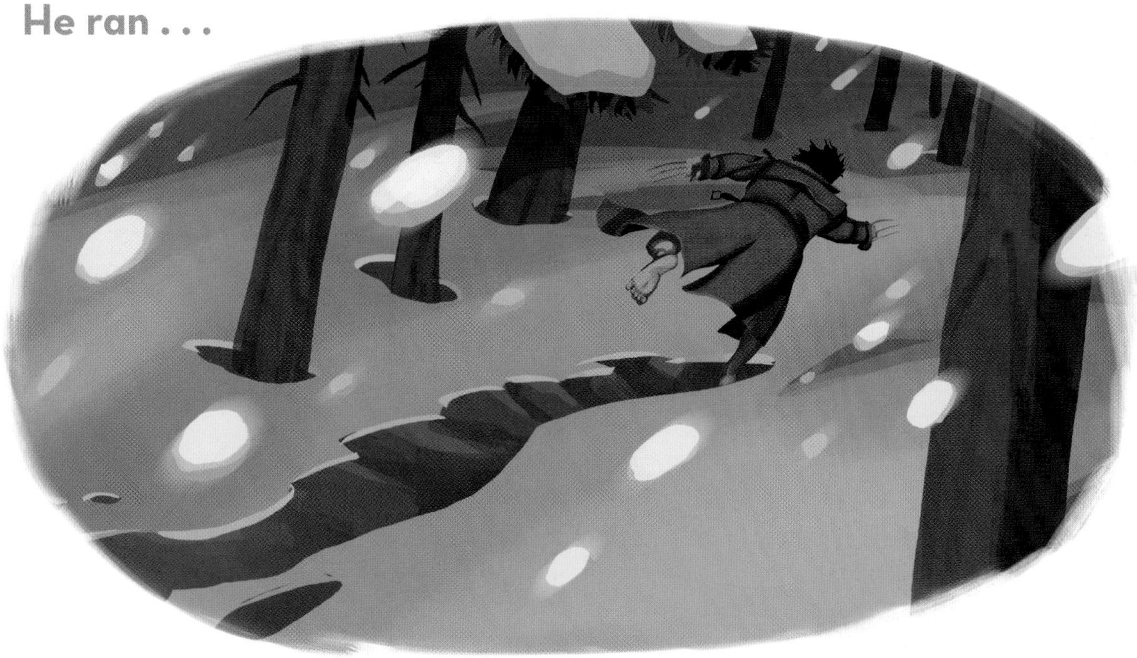

. . . and ran . . .

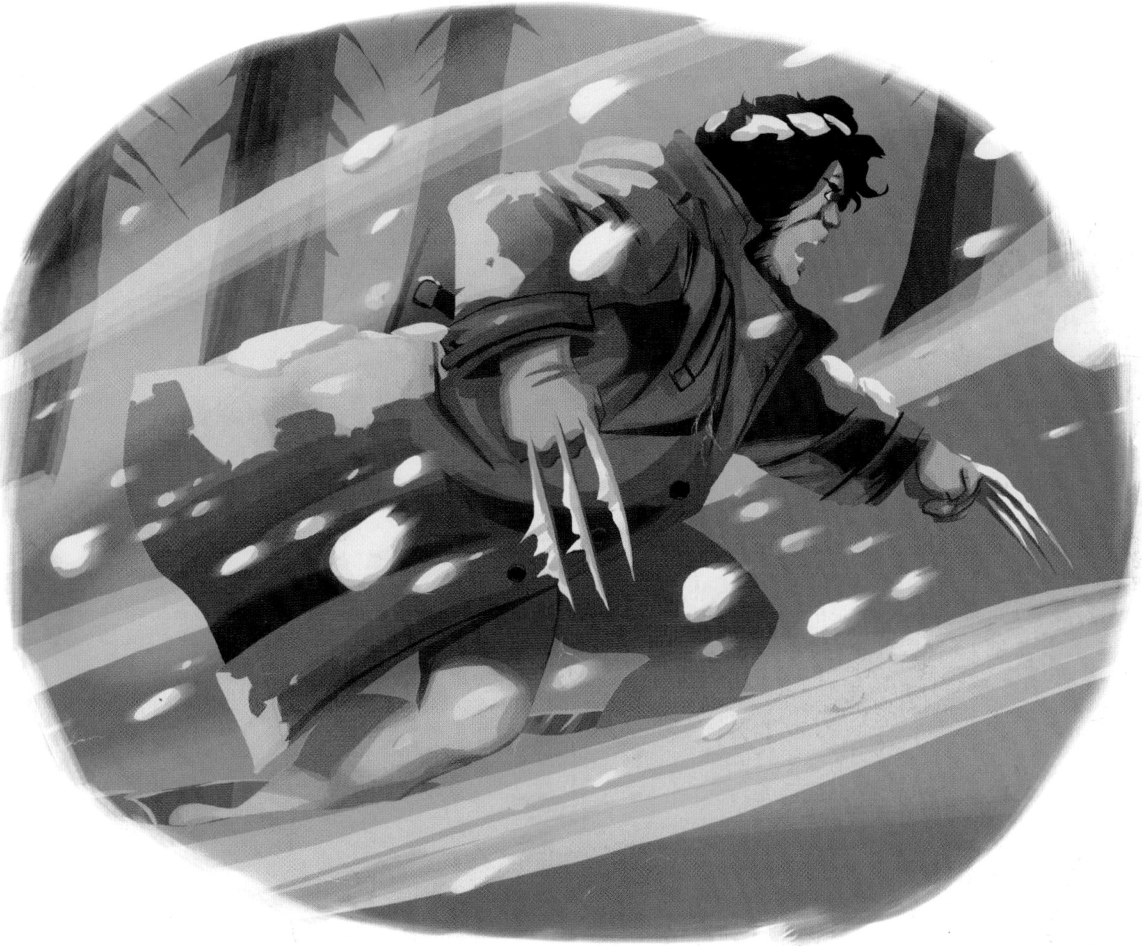

. . . until he could run
no more.

He might have **died,** if he hadn't
been found.

JAMES AND HEATHER HUDSON had found Logan and nursed him back to health.

But the only thing he could remember was his name—**Logan.**

James had been working for the government on a Super
Hero project called **Department H.** He called himself
Guardian and Heather called herself Vindicator. James
thought Logan would make a good hero, too. He gave
Logan a costume and a codename . . .

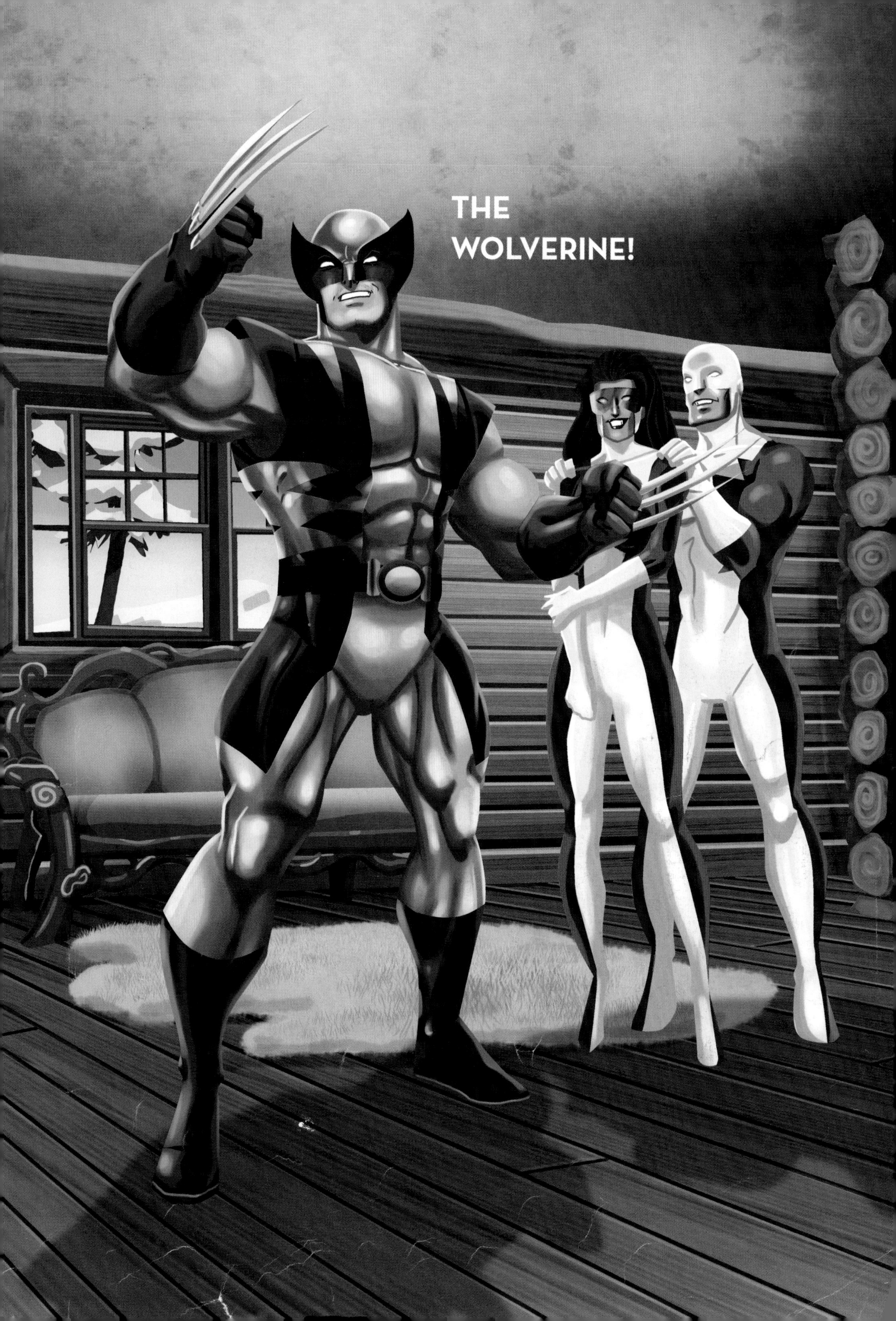

THE WOLVERINE!

Together Guardian and Wolverine formed a Super Hero team called **Alpha Flight.**

But often, Wolverine went out on missions alone.

Wolverine led Alpha Flight
into many victorious battles.
But even though he was proud
of Alpha Flight and cared
deeply for James and Heather,
he didn't feel at home.

He still felt alone.

And though he spent a
lifetime searching—

he eventually found the
family he was looking for.

He joined a **team of mutants**. Like him, they were outcasts. Each was a loner . . .

But together they were a team called the **X-MEN**.

He had been called many things—James, Logan, a Canadian hero, an X-Man—but the one thing that would never change, the one thing he would always be is

THE UNSTOPPABLE WOLVERINE!